A Roman Holiday

Godsfall, Volume 4

Adam Gaffen

Published by Adam Gaffen, Author, LLC, 2024.

Table of Contents

ADAM GAFFEN

A ROMAN HOLIDAY

A GODSFALL STORY

Published by Arima Bikia, LLC
Copyright © 2022, 2024 by Adam Gaffen
Cover Design © Adam Gaffen
All rights reserved. Except as permitted under the U.S. Copyright Act of 1976, no part of this publication may be reproduced, distributed, or transmitted in any form or by any means, or stored in a database or retrieval system, without the prior written permission of the author.
Permission is explicitly not granted for use in training large language models (LLMs), AI datasets, or anything remotely resembling machine learning. Any such use is unauthorized, unethical, and likely to earn you a personal visit from an angry angel and a mildly disappointed demon. You've been warned. The characters and events portrayed in this book are fictitious. Any similarity to persons, living or dead, is purely coincidental and not intended by the author.
For more about the author, future works, and events, please visit:
www.adamgaffenauthor.com[1]

---

1. http://www.adamgaffenauthor.com

Warning: Proceed at Your Own Risk (and preferably with coffee)

This story contains:

- Explicit sex (of the enthusiastic, immortal, seatbelt-optional variety)
- Language saltier than a sailor at a Vatican bake sale
- Alternate theology that will not pass Sunday School muster
- Blindfolds used *imaginatively*
- Crimes against fashion (RIP bespoke pantsuit, you were too stylish for this world)
- Demon-on-angel banter
- Angel-on-demon bondage
- An exorcism on aisle three
- Impersonation of actual airline staff (sorry, Melinda)
- Culinary disasters that may constitute war crimes
- Emotional support coffee
- Aerophobia, jet engines, and deeply suspicious seatbelts
- D/s dynamics with safe words like "Yes, Mistress" and "Is that a tail?"
- Mild tail action (non-prehensile, mostly affectionate)
- A BOAC jetliner with a starring role
- The kind of caricatures that make your high school yearbook look tasteful

- A sneak attack prophecy
- A surprise anniversary (and you *will* like it)
- Two immortal sapphics versus one very cranky archdemon
- And at least one ruined curtain

If any of this offends you, turn back now.

Or don't—and accept the consequences like a grown-up with good taste and a questionable sense of judgment.

A Roman Holiday

"Faith, what are you doing?"

I wasn't annoyed, but I tried to fake it. Truth was, I was bored, and Faith's promise of, "Come on, let's go have some fun!" was welcome.

We'd changed into smart outfits. Faith preferred dresses, and today she picked out an emerald-green sheath, one which brought out the stunning copper of her eyes and hugged her curves. I favored pantsuits, a relatively adventurous look for women, but one I was comfortable with. Today I chose one I'd had made for me in the city, simple black and gray vertical stripes on both the cigarette pants and jacket. My blouse was white silk, and my only concession to color was my red flats. Hats and matching purses completed our looks.

And the blindfold on me.

I was less than thrilled as she guided me out of our home. We'd had plenty of adventures outdoors, but rarely during the day, and never so close to the place we lived. We might have been immortal and virtually invulnerable to mortal weapons, but we weren't stupid.

And no matter what you might think, being discreet lesbians in 1952 Westchester County, New York, wasn't easy. Our neighbors certainly suspected, but as long as we smiled and dressed modestly, they ignored the elephant on the front lawn.

Pulling me out of the house for fun put all that at risk. Having survived the witch scares in both Europe and the

American colonies—and boy, did our timing suck there, leaving one just to get caught up in another—we were both skittish about being called out.

And that left out the fact that neither of us were human.

I was a demon, and she was an angel, or we thought we were when we met. We knew better now, but old habits, old perceptions of self, persisted. I was over seven thousand years old. Faith was older, though how much older we didn't know. Some millions of years, but time was wibbly wobbly in the Head Office.

Both our former employers utterly forbade our relationship.

We didn't care. We were the last Thirteens, and their rules didn't apply to us, no matter how much they wished they did.

So going out to have fun, with *that* tone of voice from Faith? There was a good chance we'd end up shin-deep in something smelly. That's okay; we'd dealt with repercussions before, and would again.

"I can't tell you!" she sing-songed, guiding me to our car.

"Faith," I growled, settling into the seat. We shared a beautiful new Jaguar, an XK 120 roadster, red and right-hand drive. We'd both learned to drive while living in London, and though we'd been back in the US for a couple of decades, we both preferred the UK set-up.

"It's a surprise," she said, tucking my skirt in and closing the door.

"I got that." I heard her come around and settle into the driver's seat. Then she was busy getting the car running and us out onto the road, so I held my tongue. Immortal or not, I didn't want to distract her and cause an accident. I liked that car.

I waited as patiently as I could. It was easy at first, with the grumble of the engine, the wind and sun on me, and my love next to me. I rested my hand on her thigh, just so she could feel my touch.

But when we'd been moving for at least a half-hour my patience ran out.

"Faith, where are you taking me?"

She tsked at me. "What part of surprise don't you understand?"

"Faith!"

"Oh, fine, you can take off the blindfold. For now."

I whipped the cloth from my face. We were on the parkway, headed towards the city.

"What's the big deal?" I said. "We go into the city all the time."

"Today's special. And we're not going into the city."

Again with the non-answer. I decided on a different tactic and shimmied over in the seat, pressing my thigh against hers. She dropped an arm around my shoulders and pulled me into her.

"I love you, Kalili."

"I love you, Faith, and if you tell me where we're going...?" I purred into her ear, and I felt her shiver.

"Not while I'm driving!" She laughed, and I felt her push her *taaqat* back.

Damn. She was blocking me out of her thoughts.

"Too clever by half."

"Sweetheart, you think I don't know your tricks? After all this time?"

She had a point. We'd been together since the Middle Ages, and if there was anything she didn't know about me, or vice versa? It hadn't happened yet.

"Of course you do," I said. "But what's so special about today?"

"Use that brain for something other than trying to get into my pants, Kalili."

"Hmph. Like you wear any."

She dimpled.

"A hint?"

"Hint?"

"Hint. Please."

"I like it when you beg."

"Faith!" She knew exactly what she was doing, playing with my buttons.

"I'll give you a hint. Rome."

"That's not a hint!"

We sped on, Faith with that maddening smile playing on her lips. Fine. If she wasn't going to tell me, I wasn't going to ask any longer. The skyline of the city loomed larger and larger, and then we passed it.

"Lilith take it, Faith. Where are we going?"

"The airport."

"Airport? What?"

"Airport."

I did my best to think through my confusion. Airport. Rome. She wouldn't. Would she?

"Faith, are we flying somewhere?"

Her smile blossomed. "We are. I have our tickets, and I packed a bag for us."

There were several airports in New York, so I still didn't know where we were going. Couldn't be Rome. Could it?

"Rome?"

"You remembered!"

"No, you said Rome earlier."

Her face fell, but she recovered quickly. "I did. You'll figure it out."

The rest of the drive to the airport, parking the car, getting into the terminal, all passed in a blur. I was trying to make the connection, and Faith was in charge of the details. I didn't snap back to the here-and-now until we were walking out to our plane. Which looked different.

"Faith? Honey? Are you sure this is the right plane?"

I couldn't see any engines. We were both Immortal. We had wings. We could fly over the ocean, and had before. And we could jump from place to place, as long as we knew the destination. If we didn't know the destination, we had to get there physically, and the past twenty years and the revolution in air transportation had spoiled me. I enjoyed flying when someone else had to do all the work!

This plane looked incomplete. The body, the wings, and the tail were there, but where were the propellers?

Faith didn't get what I meant. "This is the right gate, but I can ask."

We were near the stairs, and one of the air hostesses was helping the few passengers up.

"Excuse me, this is the flight to Rome?"

The young woman, cute in a cookie-cutter sort of way, smiled her hostess smile at us. "Yes, ma'am, BOAC 105."

She gestured for us to climb, but I pulled Faith back. "Where are the engines?"

The hostess heard me and the smile grew wider.

"Right there." She pointed at two oval openings in the back edge of the wing.

"No, no, those aren't engines."

The smile faltered, then resumed. "They're jet engines, ma'am."

"Jet?"

Oh, fuck no. No, no, no. I'd heard of these things. They were in the fighters that we'd dodged during the war. Belching black smoke and making a terrible noise, and Faith wanted me to trust them?

"It's perfectly safe," the hostess was saying. "Alice–"

"Who?" I was confused now.

"G-ALYS is her designation. We call her Alice. Alice is a good girl, and she'll get us across the ocean in no time. Fourteen hours from here to Rome, with stops in Newfoundland, the Azores, and Spain."

Faith tugged on my arm. "Kal, don't make a fuss. We'll be fine." She put a hint of emphasis on the last sentence, reminding me of our immortality. Even if things went sideways, we'd be fine. We might even avert a disaster.

"A jet."

"Yes, ma'am." The hostess replaced the worn smile with a new one from her inexhaustible supply. "Please. We will depart shortly."

I followed Faith up and to our seats, all the way forward behind a second air hostess. We were the only ones in the small compartment, though there were seats for eight. Big, comfortable seats, like the armchairs we had at home.

"Hello, I'm Melinda, and I'll be your hostess." This one was blonde but otherwise identical to the first two.

"Hello, Melinda. I'm Faith, and this is my friend, Kalili."

She smiled and bobbed her head. "My pleasure. We'll be taking off soon, and then I'll serve you beverages."

Melinda helped us secure ourselves, gave us a menu to examine for our dinner, then went forward to do whatever it was a hostess did when not, um. Hostessing.

"Faith, why are we flying to Rome?"

"Because I have a surprise for you."

"*This* isn't the surprise?"

"No."

She dimpled, terribly pleased with herself.

"Faith...!" I tried to be fierce, but she knew me too well.

"Hush. We're getting ready to take off." She laid her hand on mine, and our thoughts joined as our fingers intertwined. Though she still held back the surprise, whatever it was.

"I'll be good," I muttered, and her smile grew wider.

"I know it's hard, dear. But be patient."

"Patient. Angel, how long have you known me?"

"A millennium."

"Have I *ever* been patient?"

"No, dear. That's never been one of your vices."

"And why do you think I'll start now?"

"I've always been an optimist."

I was cut off by a crackling from a speaker. Then a cultivated male British voice, the kind which would weaken the knees of most females and inspire envy in males, took its place.

"Welcome aboard BOAC 105 with service to Lajes and Ciampino, Rome. I am your Captain, Nathaniel Porter, and you'll be flying in my hands. My copilot is Zachary MacDonald. Our flight engineer is Christopher Gibson, and we're all trusting the navigation abilities of Mr. Toby Thomson." He paused, and I heard a ripple of nervous laughter from the other passengers behind us. "Flight time will be eleven hours and eight minutes, with refueling stops at Gander, Lajes, and Adolfo Suarez airports extending total duration to slightly under fourteen hours."

He paused, and I heard indistinct voices in the background.

"I regret that our schedule—" He pronounced it with the soft sh of the English. "—Will not permit disembarkation at our stop in Gander for anyone not ticketed as their destination. Though, and no offense to the poor bloke leaving us there, Gander's a nasty piece of nowhere. And it's bloody cold." More titters from behind me.

"Though Lajes is beautiful any time of the year," Porter added, and Faith looked at me meaningfully. We had spent the better part of two months there, back in the early fifteenth century, until settlement had become too earnest. We may have inadvertently contributed to the mermaid legends in the area.

Possibly.

It was a blissful time.

My reminiscing was cut off by Porter' continuing, but the echo of the memory reverberated between my mind and Faith's.

"Expected take-off is ten twenty-two local time, with arrival in Rome at seven-thirty tomorrow morning. For those on your first flight, welcome, and don't worry, we shan't permit you to miss any meals. Our cabin attendants, Misses Spencer, Black, and Cunningham in the rear, and Miss Ward in the fore, will ensure your complete comfort. And now, ladies and gentlemen, I regret I must return to our preparations. Ta!"

With that, he clicked off, and Melinda—Miss Ward, apparently—returned. She saw our clasped hands and said nothing, merely giving us a knowing half-smile, and I relaxed a hair. I didn't want to borrow any trouble we didn't need to have.

"Did you ladies decide on a drink?"

A thousand years of experience, and our connected minds, meant I didn't have to look at Faith.

"Coffee, please. Black for me, cream and sugar for my companion."

"Very good, Ms....?" She left the question hanging for me to answer, or not. I'd adopted many surnames over the years, and none of them meant anything to me.

"Keoka. But call me Kalili, please." I could be gracious. I could!

"Very good, Kalili. Then you must be Ms. Burrows?" Melinda asked Faith, who nodded in return.

"Please, I can hardly have you call me Ms. Burrows if you're calling my friend Kalili. I'm Faith."

The name seemed to register in Melinda's mind, but she didn't say anything other than, "Of course. I shall return presently."

We chatted about inanities, as all our true communication was done wordlessly, until our coffee arrived. Two mugs, half-full. At my questioning look, Melinda explained.

"We only have a few moments before we take off," she said. "I shall bring you full cups after we're airborne."

"Thank you." I hadn't considered it and was grateful she had. She didn't leave as I expected her to. Instead, she said, "Faith?"

My blonde beauty turned her full attention to Melinda. This was blatantly unfair. Nobody had resisted Faith's personality since the thirteenth century.

"Yes, Melinda?"

"Are you the cartoonist? The one who wrote *Flapper Filosofy*?"

She was, and I restrained a groan. My beloved, always trying to enlighten humanity, had created the cartoon to influence equality between the sexes. She drew flappers, the independent women prevalent in the 1920's, in a way that encouraged experimentation and free thinking. It had a successful run before she dropped it in the mid-thirties.

"I am," Faith answered. She'd never learned how to lie, saying it was my specialty.

Melinda's face lit up. "My mother had an enormous collection of your cartoons, and I loved looking at them when I was little."

Faith returned the smile. "That's very kind of you. I'm glad they brought you such joy."

Melinda was too star-struck to say anything else and floated away.

"I knew that cartoon would be trouble," I growled.

"Hush. She's a fan, that's all."

I didn't reply, but picked up my coffee and took a sip. It was exquisite.

"Much better than calda, or even the buna we had. Remember that? That Ethiope on the bank—" I jerked, nearly spilling it my cup. "That's the surprise!"

Faith's smile was pleased and rueful. "I knew you'd figure it out eventually. Yes, love. I'm taking you to Rome for our anniversary."

"Has it been a full millennium?" I sipped, concealing my glee. I'd guessed it!

"It has. In two days."

"Will Avy be joining us?"

Our other *arima bikia*, Avareth, the demon who'd been my minder and lover, spent as much time with us as she could. Her duties in Hell kept her busy, though, so her participation wasn't a given.

"If she can, she will, but that anniversary is a few months from now, if we're being precise."

I nodded. "What's the plan?"

Faith sighed. She'd done well to resist to this point, but now that I had an inkling? I'd ask her until she gave in. Or she could surrender gracefully. "I want to retrace our first days," she said, surrendering. "Van's palace, as much of old Rome as we can find, the town on the coast, Ravenna, all of it."

I whistled quietly. "Not much left after a thousand years."

"Maybe, but we ought to track it down."

I knew what she meant. Every Immortal had an aura and left a trace wherever they went. These faded after time, but the being who left the trace could always detect it. Then I had a thought.

"Rome's even worse than when we were there, Faith." Rome had never been a good city, between the thugs and brigands and murderers and rapists, and when you got out of the politicians and got into the general population, it only got worse. As for Immortals, it was less neutral ground and more a free-for-all. We could handle ourselves, but I'd rather not use any of our powers if I didn't absolutely have to.

"I thought of that. Thakumis' Blade is in my purse."

I sighed in relief. The Blade was ancient, but it was the last remnant of a former Prince of Hell and deadly to any Immortal. With that, we wouldn't have to rely on any of our powers to survive. The only drawback was its tendency to possess the mind of whoever wielded it. Faith and I, combined, could force it out of my mind, and over the centuries, it had stopped trying.

Mostly.

I still felt better knowing it was near.

I tried not to pay attention to the hydraulic whines as the doors were closed, the clunks and whirrs as turbines were brought to power, and the jerks as the plane was pulled to the runway. Faith picked up on my nerves and invited me into her mind, a much more tranquil place, and I happily accepted.

Takeoff was uneventful, and we were soon cruising northward.

"Ladies, are you ready for lunch?" It was our friendly hostess, with two covered trays. I was suddenly aware of the scanty breakfast I'd had and the time elapsed, and a growl escaped my stomach.

"I'll take that as a yes," she said, setting the trays down. I had to admit the food smelled good, and it only improved when she removed the covers.

We had shrimp cocktails, a Caesar salad, and the main course of roasted chicken with the usual sides and sauces. Completing the meals were glasses of white wine and sparkling water.

"Isn't this better than flying?" Faith asked.

I had to nod, having just filled my mouth. One of Faith's occasional vocations was as a waitress. Though she swore it wasn't true, I remained convinced there was a school to train them, and one skill they taught was asking questions when the customer's mouth was full.

Captain Porter made occasional announcements when we passed notable locations, but we mostly ignored him. In a short time, we were descending to land in Gander, our first stop.

I'll admit it; I clutched Faith's hand until the wheels were on the ground and we'd slowed to little more than running speed. That was the highlight, or lowlight, of our visit to Gander. Porter wasn't wrong. When they opened the door to let off the one unlucky bastard deplaning, a cold gust ran the length of the plane.

"I'll bring you more coffee after we lift off again, ladies," Melinda said while we were on the ground, then left us alone. I returned to an earlier topic.

"I still can't believe it's been a thousand years. Doesn't seem like it. Oh, crap. There's that stupid prophecy, isn't there?"

Faith nodded. She was better at keeping records than me.

She quoted: "A thousand years will the Thirteens roam the world before their Destiny calls to them. A millennium of peace before the Contest resumes. Then shall they take their place and rule."

"Ah, fuck." I didn't want to rule the cosmos. Faith didn't either. Which, of course, is why we were the ones chosen to do so. When we united, we were a goddess, more powerful than any of the three siblings who created the universe, created the Thirteens, created the Contest. It was an oversight on Lucifer and the Maker's part and the reason we were the last Thirteens in existence.

Faith squeezed my hand. "I'm still looking for a loophole."

I'd actively avoided thinking about this particular prophecy. It didn't seem to bode well for us. But now, with the sounds of engines and airplane noises around us, I needed something to distract me.

It worked. I almost didn't notice the takeoff and the whining climb to altitude, the popping sounds as the fuselage pressurized, or the groans of stressed metals.

Almost.

After our full coffees had been brought to us, along with biscuits, good ones, I mumbled around a mouthful, "Faith."

"Don't talk with your mouth full of anything but me," Faith said, and I shivered. "What?"

"The prophecy."

"Yes?"

"Tell it to me again."

She did, and I chuckled.

"What?"

"I found your loophole. The first line and the second line."

"What about them?" Faith's forehead wrinkled in concentration, a mannerism I still found unbearably cute.

"It's not the same thousand years."

"What? No, of course it is."

I scoffed. "You think there's been a thousand years of peace? Do you want to count wars, crusades, or just revolutions?"

"Well, there's been peace between Below and the Head Office. We've made sure of that."

I nodded. It had kept us busy, but she was correct. The Contest had been reduced to paperwork wars and subtle attempts at corruption and redemption.

"What words are used? In the original, that is."

"A thousand years? *Kiloa chronia.*" Many of the prophecies we'd uncovered had been written in Greek. Why? We couldn't get a straight answer from Ariel, and Hell's records were a mess.

"And a millennium?"

"*Kilotia.* Fuck me sideways, you're right!"

I think I might have glowed. Faith was definitely the brain between us, far better at matters of scholarship than I was. It was rare I could make a coup like this.

"And we both know that it's the original wording that counts. They're not the same, Faith. We get to wander, and then there's a thousand years of peace." Another thought struck me. "Hell, Faith, there might even be time between the two periods! It doesn't say there isn't, right?"

"No..."

"So?" I was triumphant. "You're the one who keeps saying prophecies are slippery things. There are two numbers in that damn thing, but two other places where time is implied but not specified. We could have thousands of years yet!"

I leaned over and kissed her before she could protest. After a brief hesitation, she returned my kiss, our tongues greeting each other.

The humans? Faith asked, still kissing me.

Fuck 'em.

I felt her ripple of humor. *That's not what we usually do, but I suppose we could make an exception...*

Wench. You're all I want, my arima bikia.

As ever, when I used those words when in communion with Faith, we joined as fully and utterly as two beings could. So complete was our merger that we were a single entity, a goddess, encompassing all of creation. Our union was brief and timeless.

I broke the kiss with an unexpected frown.

"I felt it too," Faith said, our passions cooled. "Who?"

I shook my head. "I didn't get that. But another Immortal is on this plane, masking their aura, and I don't think they want to wish us a happy anniversary."

Suddenly, our vacation wasn't as much fun.

As the last Thirteens, we had powers far beyond other Immortals when united. As Kalili and Faith, we were more limited. When joined, we knew anything we wanted. If we focused on it, we kept the knowledge when we parted. But we had to know what we were looking for, in the tide of the universe flooding our mind. Faith had once likened it to showering under Niagara Falls, and having done it, I agreed.

Which left us with our inherent abilities.

As Kalili and Faith, we were fully telepathic with each other, whether or not we were in contact. A thousand years with your beloved did that. That gave us a means of communication others lacked. We shared the same link with Avareth when we were all in the same realm.

A skill we retained from our previous existences as angel and demon was touch-telepathy. As Thirteens, we could penetrate any mental shielding erected by an Immortal, but it wasn't subtle. More like smashing a window with a brick. They'd know they were exposed, and while neither of us worked for a particular side any longer, we didn't want to put the mortal passengers and crew at risk.

Unfortunately, subtle wasn't our strong suit.

How were we going to find the hidden Immortal without letting on we were searching for them?

We fell back to our normal abilities. Physical contact would show us the Immortal. Now, we just had to figure out a reason to touch everyone aboard.

Easy.

Not so much.

We could mingle with the other passengers, but direct contact?

Men didn't touch strange women.

Women wore gloves.

The first hour of that long leg, Gander to the Azores, was spent in silent planning. At length we came up with a plan, ran through possibilities, and then spent a few moments deciding to jump.

Ready?

When am I ever? I answered.

Faith didn't reply.

We were going to play on Faith's fading notoriety as an illustrator and offer every passenger a personalized, individual sketch. From experience, we knew Faith could rattle one off in a couple of minutes if she used some tricks we'd picked up along the way. There were forty-two people aboard, and we had a little more than three hours to land. Just enough time to reach everyone.

The contact would come when I, acting as her agent, made the official deal. No cost, of course, simply a handshake agreement not to use the art commercially. If that failed, well, Faith would find a reason to touch them while drawing, adjusting their arm or hand or the position of their neck. Something.

It was as good as we had, so we began.

Melinda gave me a wary look when I stood and balanced against the subtle motion of the airplane. I smiled and turned the full force of my charm on her.

"We want to do something for our fellow passengers," I explained. Faith stood and pulled down her bag.

"Oh?" She was curious, but not objecting. It was a start.

"Yes, if it's okay for us to move around?"

"There's no regulation against it," Melinda hedged. "But do be careful."

I turned the smile up to dazzling. "We will."

We had about two hours before we would begin preparations for landing, and we needed every minute. Faith and I scoured the aisles. I introduced her to everyone, and I could feel Faith wince with every new breach of her anonymity. Many remembered her drawings and were thrilled to have their likeness in a sketch.

And then Faith had to draw while I chatted up the next people.

Repeatedly.

My fingers are getting tired, Faith complained about halfway through.

That's not what you were saying last night.

She blushed, the rims of her ears reddening.

That was the highlight of our efforts.

We collapsed back into our seats with about ten minutes to spare.

"Nothing?" My voice was barely above a whisper. The engines were loud enough to drown out words more than a few feet away, but our compartment wasn't that big. I didn't need to do mental surgery on Melinda if she heard too much.

"Nothing," Faith confirmed. She'd done most of the touching, adjusting poses and positions. "Not a single Immortal. Two fae pretending to be human. Elves, I think."

I nodded. "Caught that. Very cute." I didn't mention that the male had given us both a thorough examination. Under different circumstances, we might have invited him home for a while.

"But no Immortals. Damn it, Kalili, I know there's one on the plane!"

"You know I don't believe in coincidences, but they happen. What if they're hiding from us?"

"Us? Why would they hide from us?" Faith seemed honestly shocked by the suggestion.

"Last of the Thirteens? We're not exactly concealing our auras, are we?" Over the years, we'd debated concealment versus openness. If we stayed hidden, and masked our auras all the time, we'd pretty well go unnoticed. But there were problems. What did we show to the world? Angel and demon? We'd attract attention from Below and the Head Office, just the routine harassment, but annoying. Human? We'd be targets.

Then again, showing our true auras, the auras of the only Thirteens, was equally risky. Did you want to talk about targets? It would be like walking around downtown Hiroshima in August of '45. Bad, bad idea.

For a while, we stayed hidden, as we honed our skills and practiced our powers. Once we had full command of them, we dropped the pretense. If there was an Immortal who could take us on together, we'd yet to meet them.

I reached that conclusion, and my head snapped up.

"Faith, what the fuck are we worrying about? We took down Gabriel, we took down Lucifer, and neither of those mosswipes are on the plane."

"You outtalked Lucifer into a deal he regrets every day, and it took both of us to handle Gabriel. An Immortal who's concealing their aura is up to something. It might not involve us, but are you willing to let any of these people suffer? Besides, aren't you just the tiniest bit curious?"

She had me, and the smirk showed she knew it.

"Fine. So who's left?"

"Crew. Pilots, navigator, engineer, and stewardesses."

"Do you think you can charm your way into the cockpit?" I asked, knowing the answer.

"Go ahead, Kalili," she said with a resigned smile. "I've never been partial to men. I can charm the stewardesses."

"After we take off again?"

"Agreed."

She leaned into me, and we didn't need any more words.

Landing wasn't any more fun in the Azores than Gander. It was warmer, though, and we took advantage of the fading daylight to wander as far afield as we could in the ninety minutes we had. As befitted ladies, we had our purses with us, and I felt the whisper of the Blade from Faith's calling to me.

"Faith?"

We were holding hands, but we'd perfected the art of keeping our thoughts our own when we chose. We relished our mergers, but we also needed time and space to be ourselves.

"Kal?"

"Thank you." I leaned over to kiss the corner of her mouth. "This was a sweet idea."

"I didn't expect to go Immortal-hunting," she groused before relenting. "I wanted to do something really special."

"You gave me the chance to be the person I am." I pulled her close, heedless of what any of our fellow passengers might think.

"How sweet." The voice came from ahead of us, but we couldn't see anyone. I recognized it, though Faith was faster.

"Melinda."

"Show yourself," I demanded, and Melinda laughed. She must be one of those rare humans who could use magik.

"And give you an advantage?" Now the voice was beside me and I whirled, hand itching for the Blade. "Not likely."

And now she was on Faith's side. Damn her.

We stood back-to-back, shuffling in a small circle.

"The Thirteens." There was scorn in Melinda's tone. "Cowering like a couple of humans. What's wrong? Afraid of me?"

"No, but we don't want to scar their minds." Faith gestured to the passengers milling around the plane, and the airport workers going about their tasks. "Using our powers isn't subtle."

"Push me, Melinda, see how many fucks I have left to give," I growled.

"What shocking language!"

Can you get a fix on her?

No. She's good, Faith answered with a mental snarl. Fine. I could be subtle.

"Melinda, let's talk about this like rational beings."

No response.

Head for the plane. Maybe she won't try anything if we get close. Long shot. But Faith started moving towards Alice.

"Stop."

Fuck. She noticed, and she dropped her invisibility. "I don't give a damn about these meatsacks. Go ahead. Any who get killed are on you, you know." Melinda ran her hands along her sides, and I knew what she was, even if I didn't know the who.

"How about you tell me who you are? Hiding behind Melinda's face? Possession is so passé."

"Well done, little demoness." Melinda's voice changed, getting rougher and deeper, and I knew who it was.

"Onnirrech. What an unpleasant surprise." I'd killed him a millennium before. At least, I'd thought I'd killed him. Current evidence suggested that the archdemon's death hadn't been as permanent as I'd hoped. "What rock have you been hiding under all these years?"

"Ah, yes. Your sense of humor. I haven't missed it."

"And I haven't missed you." I felt Faith moving, and then the Blade was pressed into my palm. I brandished it. "Let's fix that again."

"Where have you been?" Faith said, a note of curiosity in her voice.

"Where I'm about to send you. The Outer Darkness."

Now my curiosity was aroused. I waggled the Blade, taking another step toward the plane. "Go on."

"Why should I?" She feinted forward, dancing back out of my reach as I swiped at her. "And the Blade won't work on this body, not like it does on Immortals."

Fuck. I was afraid of that. Which meant I'd have to kill Melinda's body to get Onnirrech out of her, a deal I wasn't sure she'd appreciate.

I spread my arms wide. "Then talk. Maybe we can make a deal. It wasn't anything personal. Killing you, that is."

Another step.

"Not personal?" he bellowed, the rage out of place in the blonde body. "You destroyed my body with a single cut and cast my soul out of this plane! Do you have any idea how hard it is to return from the Outer Dark? How many deals I made? How much I owe to the entities who assisted me in my painful journey back to this reality? Of course you don't. But I'm going to give you the chance to find out!"

This time, it wasn't a feint. She slammed into me and knocked me to the tarmac, the Blade skittering away. I'd forgotten about the metabolic supercharge a possessed human got from their passenger. Onnirrech wasn't as strong as he'd been as an archdemon, but he was far stronger than Melinda's body should have been.

His hands, with their perfect, professional nails, wrapped around my throat and clenched. I brought my arms between his and smashed outward, lifting my head to slam into Melinda's forehead with a crack. Whoever survived would feel that later.

I rolled away from him, bringing my legs under to leap to my feet, but he tackled me from behind and drove me back to the ground. I heard bones break.

A surge of *taaqat* into me told me Faith had joined the battle. Onnirrech screamed. I scrabbled away before turning to look at what Faith had done.

She was riding Melinda's back, legs wrapped around his waist, pinning his arms to his sides.

Kalili! Get him out of her!

"How?" My head hurt too much to transmit to her.

You'll have to go in and pull him out.

Leave my body?

Oh, fuck. This wasn't going to be fun.

"On it. Hold him!" *And catch me when I fall*, I thought.

Then I was charging at them, wrapping them both in my arms and then it was all about my soul.

The souls of Immortals were maintained by their *taaqat*. What we'd learned, accidentally, is that a soul can ride the flow of *taaqat* from one body to another and separate from its home body.

What Faith was suggesting was I drag Onnirrech's soul from Melinda's body into mine.

Fine. I could do that.

What the fuck she was planning after that? I had no clue, but she was my *arima bikia*. I was all in.

Leaving my body was frighteningly easy. As my last shreds of consciousness passed into Melinda, I felt Faith extend herself into my body to maintain it in my absence and keep it empty. Otherwise, I might return with two battles on my hands: Onnirrech and an unknown intruder.

Onnirrech was everywhere inside Melinda's body. I sensed his presence all through her, controlling even the smallest aspect of her being, but she was still there. Submerged beneath his soul, but there, and fighting.

I wasn't going to give up if she hadn't.

Onnirrech! Get out of here now and I won't drag your sorry dead ass out!

Fuck you, Kalili! His soul was black, blacker even than I expected from an archdemon. He was consumed by hate, yes, but more than that. There were the debt markers of dozens, hundreds, of other souls pocking it, dragging on him.

Your choice.

Stupid demon. I don't know how you've stayed alive with that angel for so long, but it ends today! In here, you don't have that damnable blade, and I'm the stronger!

He didn't know.

I'd killed him before the message that I was a Thirteen got to him. All he knew was he was ordered to kill an angel. A thousand years earlier, I was a bonus, but we were just a job.

I was tempted to play with him. Ooh, I was tempted. I was stronger than him as a being of pure *taaqat*, but I tamped it down. Leaving my body for any length of time was risky, and the risks increased every second.

Best to get this done quickly, then.

I latched onto his soul.

Stupid demon, he repeated, reaching with tendrils of his soul to crush me. I swatted them away and tugged. He was thoroughly woven into Melinda's body, but one thread at a time I pried him loose and cut him off.

You can't do this! I'm an archdemon! he wailed, fear striking deep.

And I'm a Thirteen, motherfucker. You're coming with me!

I pulled.

He fought, he struggled, he clung to his hold on Melinda with desperation, but I was stronger. More, I was pissed. I was not about to let him waltz in and take over a human. I wasn't a superhero, but I had a soul and a conscience.

I kept pulling, disengaging him from Melinda, and wrapping his being in mine. This gave him an idea, and he started hammering at my being, but I'd expected it and easily rebuffed his attacks.

An indefinable chunk of eternity later, I had all of Onnirrech pried from Melinda and encapsulated in my essence. I withdrew from the human with a final intangible reassurance to her that, yes, everything would be alright and someone would explain it to her. Then I turned my attention back to Onni.

He was fighting. Hard. I could feel each attack as if it were a physical blow, and they stung.

Faith, I've got the fucker, now what?

Faith settled an unconscious Melinda to the ground before she answered.

Hold him.

That's your plan? Fuck me. Oof! Onni hit me with a punishing attack, sensing my distraction. I closed my eyes and concentrated inward.

Just hold him for a little longer, she begged. *I know you can.*

I turned my attention back to Onnirrech. Maybe if I squeezed he'd be a little less frisky? I didn't have any idea how to do it, but that had never stopped me in the past. I visualized my *taaqat* as a glowing ball, completely enveloping Onnirrech's scarred soul. Then I compressed it.

Stop it! He pushed against me, but I held the advantage, and I inexorably shrank his space.

I'll leave, you win, just let me go!

Not a chance. I'm going to make sure you're done for good this time.

I didn't have a clue how I was going to do it, but I meant every word.

I know. I think. Faith joined my efforts, and Onni's space shrank dramatically.

Great, I huffed, or I would have had I been speaking. *How?*

Trust me.

That was the trump card, and I immediately acceded. *What do you need me to do?*

Join with me.

I opened my eyes in near-panic. We weren't that far from the plane and passengers, and I didn't know what we'd look like joined. I'd never looked at our bodies when we'd been in union.

Faith?

Trust me, she repeated. I did.

I opened myself wholly to her, leaving only a tiny portion of my awareness to monitor Onni's prison, and we were One.

"Onnirrech, archdemon of Hell, you are banished from this existence for all time, never to return, condemned by your actions to wander the cosmos alone. None shall ever see, hear, sense, or feel you again. Begone," I/We said.

There was a soundless shriek as Onnirrech's soul was cast out of its prison and into eternity, swiftly cut off as Our curse took effect.

Then Faith returned to her self, and our momentary eternity of godhood broke.

"Damn," I said, bending to rest my hands on my knees. "What did we just do?"

I knew what we did, but the meaning of it eluded me.

"An impromptu exorcism, I think. It felt similar to what we've done before, but different." Faith wrinkled her nose. This was one of her mannerisms I still found irresistible.

"You think?"

"When we're One, Our will overrides anything as trivial as natural laws. We think it, it is. You know that." Faith knelt by Melinda, checking her pulse. I joined her. If we needed to heal her, it would be best if we both contributed.

"Yeah, but is that it? He's gone?"

"As gone as we can make him. Ah, Melinda." Faith's tone switched immediately to concern. "How are you feeling?"

"Quite odd," the stewardess admitted. "What am I doing out here?"

"We rather hoped you could tell us," I said, slipping into a more English mode of speech easily. "What's the last thing you remember?"

"Fetching you coffee and biscuits after Gander?" She sounded unsure, and I wasn't surprised. Having the soul of a long-dead archdemon occupy your body for a few hours had that effect.

"Anything after that?" Faith pressed.

"Nothing clearly," she said, sitting up with Faith's help. "It all goes foggy, I'm afraid."

I jumped in, guessing that her next question would be one we didn't want to answer. I'd always been better at lying than Faith.

"You seemed fine, at least until we landed and you left the plane. We were worried about you, so followed you until you collapsed. Fainted, I guess." I pressed my hand to her arm and fixed my creative version of events into her mind.

"Yes, I must have. It's been a long day, after all." The ability of humans to accept the illogical changes in their world and rationalize them away continued to astonish me.

"Let's get you back," I said, putting an arm around Melinda's waist and lifting her as easily as I would a toddler. "We have a little while before we take off again. Maybe that will be enough."

Faith wrapped her arm from the other side, and between us, we sent a steady trickle of our *taaqats* into Melinda. By the time we'd reached the stairs up to the fuselage, she could walk on her own.

"Mel!" It was the cookie-cutter blonde hostess who had greeted us. She dashed to Melinda's side, clinging to her. Faith and I shared a look. We knew how she felt.

"I'm okay, Gillian," Mel said, putting her hands on the blonde's cheeks and pulling her close for a quick, discrete kiss. "Kalili and Faith helped me."

"You naughty girl, you had me worried. I came forward to find you for our, ah, our meeting, and you'd gone." Gillian flashed a nervous look at us both, and I did my best to reassure her with my eyes that we understood and wouldn't give their secret away.

I succeeded.

"I don't know what happened," Melinda admitted. "And I'm not sure I'm in any shape to tend the cabin for the last leg."

Oh, this wasn't good. Time to step in.

"We don't need anything, Melinda. Really. I'm sure Gillian can show us how to make coffee, and you can tell us where those biscuits are, and we'll be fine."

"Yes, and I'll come to check on you," Gillian added, relief in her voice. "You're sure, Miss Kalili?"

"Just Kalili," I laughed. "And I've been fending for myself for a long time. Ouch!"

Faith looked innocently at me and pretended she hadn't stomped on my toes.

"Then if you ladies will excuse us?" Gillian said. "We have a small sleeping cabin, and I'll install Mel there before we take off, make excuses to the Captain, and get all this straightened out. Come on, Mel."

She took Mel's arm and placed it on her shoulder. Side-by-side, the two made their way up the stairs, Melinda leaning intimately on Gillian.

"Very cute," I said. "Reminds me of us."

The next bit passed uneventfully enough. Faith helped Melinda settle in for a rest, behind a door in the galley we hadn't noticed.

"Crew rest," Gillian explained as she gave me a crash course in the galley's operation. She was a whirlwind.

"Convenient," I said.

"Quite." She dimpled, obviously remembering some other uses for the tiny space before regaining her composure.

"Pity there's nothing like that for us passengers."

"Oh, there is. Your seats will recline fully, and if you require a bit more space, the seat arm will fold down so you can be closer. There's also a curtain you can draw to prevent excessive light." Her cheeks reddened at her presumption, and I smiled.

"Very kind. Yes, Faith and I enjoy closeness." That was enough, and she relaxed.

"I'll be busy in the main cabin, so if you'd prefer, I'll close the cabin door. So you can rest," she added with a hint of humor.

"That's most thoughtful. Yes, resting would be good."

She nodded briskly, and we were back to details.

Faith reappeared, closing the door and standing next to me. My practice with the compact kitchen was meeting with limited success.

"I'll just pop in and check on Melinda," Gillian said and ducked through the door.

"How is she?"

Faith rested her hand on my arm for a moment, searching my thoughts for the information Gillian had tried to impart, then started helping. "She doesn't remember anything clearly. She thinks she dreamed it. That's probably as good as we're liable to get."

"As long as she doesn't dig too deep." I had an ugly thought. "Could Onnirrech have left a back door? A way to return to her? He was never much for planning, but I don't want to assume he didn't and get bitten in the ass."

"I didn't see anything like that." The timer dinged and Faith opened the oven. She pulled out the pan and peeled back the foil. A plume of smoke wafted upward. "What is this supposed to be?"

"Pork chops."

Faith tilted the pan.

"Not any longer." She binned them. "I think we keep you away from cooking for the rest of the flight."

"Hmph. Still... I think we ought to stay in touch with Melinda. After."

Faith accepted my change in the subject. "Agreed. Invite them over? When they're in New York next?"

I nodded. "Gillian too?"

"They're a pair; I don't think we'll get one without the other."

"Just making sure you picked up on it, too. Oh, Gillian told me…"

I relayed the news about our potential comfort and privacy for the next leg, and Faith grinned.

"I was wondering how long you were going to last."

"Hey!" I protested, smiling back.

We restored the galley to a semblance of order before Gillian re-emerged. If her cap was askew, neither of us were going to comment.

"I can't thank you two enough for what you did," she gushed. "Melinda is, well, we're closer than family. If anything were to happen to her, I don't know what I'd do."

I reached out and straightened her hat. "We understand," I assured her. Gillian nodded once, then was proper and terribly British again.

"Now, I must return to my duties. We shall lift in twenty minutes. I shall close the door between the cabins when I go, and as I am the only one with a key, you shan't be disturbed."

Another nod and she was gone. The door closed with a click, then a second as she secured it from the other side.

Faith was in my arms before the echoes died away.

"I love you, you good-hearted demon," she murmured against my lips.

"And I love you, my wicked angel." Her tongue tapped against my lips, and I gently caressed it with my tongue, my hands roaming over her clothes.

"I want you," she said when my tongue finished playing.

"What's stopping you?" I bent to nibble on her earlobe, trailing kisses down the nape of her neck.

"Nothing," she admitted, fingers working the buttons of my outfit for a moment. "Screw this."

"Faith, wait…!"

Too late. She grasped the lapels of my smart pantsuit and pulled. The fabric, buttons, and zippers didn't stand a chance. One button pinged off the low cabin roof, and another thunked into the door.

"Dammit, Faith, that was a bespoke suit!" I grumped, but I didn't have any heat to it. After all, she'd cut through all the time-consuming parts, and all I had left was a revealing set of lingerie: a bra that was more lace than anything else, the smallest, skimpiest panties I owned, and green garters.

"Better. And I'll get you a new one." She put her hands on my breasts and teased my nipples into alertness.

"I think, before I do anything to you, we need to figure out these seats, otherwise we're going to do some interesting acrobatics." She giggled at this. "What?"

"Like we did in the park two weeks ago?" she said, leaning down to kiss the exposed flesh above the lace.

Our little Jaguar was a wonderful car, one of the finest we'd ever owned, but it didn't have a back seat. Or much headroom. When we'd gotten a little carried away with a necking session, we'd ended up twisted around each other and incorporating various levers into our contortions.

"Yes, like that. Stop it, Faith. For now," I hastily amended. I turned to examine the seats and felt Faith's hand on the skin of my thigh. "You're not helping."

"I'm helping myself," she retorted. But she withdrew her hand and between us, we figured out the reclining mechanism.

I stepped back to look at our handiwork and frowned. "I wonder how we move that table. Faith, no!"

There was a popping sound, the rivets giving way, and Faith moved the now-detached table over to the other side of the cabin. "What? I can put it back, good as new."

I rolled my eyes. Then she was pressed against me, her arms wrapping me tight, and any concern for the table went away.

"You're overdressed," I complained, feeling the smooth silk of her dress under my hands.

"Don't you dare," she hissed. "Besides, it's my turn."

"Your turn for what?"

"Mistress," Faith growled, biting my collarbone almost hard enough to draw blood. I gasped at the exquisite pleasure and pain.

"Yes, Mistress," I whispered.

"Good girl. Lie down."

I climbed onto the seat and stretched.

"Arms," Faith demanded, and I held them in front of me, a shiver of anticipation running through me. She maneuvered them behind the seat and tied them together with a leg of my ruined suit.

"What are you going to do, Mistress?" Questions were allowed, and the partner had to answer. We'd worked out the rules for our play centuries earlier.

"You'll see."

But she didn't have to provide useful answers. Dammit.

I watched as she rested her hand on the curtain that would give us privacy, then changed her mind. Instead, she picked up the other leg of my trousers and blindfolded me. Again.

"Faith, what are you doing?" At least the fabric was comfortable against my skin. I could free myself if I chose. Nothing mortal could hold me for long, but it was part of the game to feign helplessness.

"Blindfolding you. Hush now, no more questions."

I stretched the senses of my body as far as I could, straining for hints.

"Be good," Faith purred in my right ear, fingers leaving electric trails down my torso. "No cheating. Do you remember our first time?"

I could answer this. "Yes." The memory was etched in my mind. It was the first time we'd become One, our first night of freedom.

"What did you tell me?" She'd moved to my left ear and licked.

I thought I knew what she meant. "I said, "Don't worry about doing. Just be." Right?" I snuck the question in, but she didn't quite answer.

"Enjoy what I'm going to do to you."

That was a command I was perfectly willing to obey.

She didn't use anything but her lips for the first minutes, placing kisses all across my body, moving silently between one kiss and the next. I never knew where she would be next, and it became a game of exquisite torture, as I tried to guess. I could feel the spots Faith kissed radiating heat, making connections, until my body was burning for her and I was groaning in anticipation.

The Captain's voice announced our departure and other trivia, but I barely registered it. Faith's fingers took over for her mouth, one or two at a time, tracing patterns on my skin and leaving trails of goosebumps in their wake.

"I'm not buckled in," I whispered. "We'll get in trouble."

"I'll keep you safe," Faith said, and she climbed on top of me, pressing me against the seat. Somewhere, somehow, she'd shed her dress and lingerie, and her bare skin on mine was tormenting with my hands tied. She reached for the sides of the seat and grabbed on, then hooked her feet over my legs and the edge.

"See?" She laid kisses on my shoulders, my neck, my throat, and I lost track of everything except the feel of her body on mine. I was intensely aware of every inch of her, and I could tell she was enjoying this as much as I. Her nipples, firm and erect, pushed against me.

Somewhere in there we took off, but I have no idea when. My world was Faith.

Faith paralleled the plane's climb to altitude, bringing me closer and closer to climax even as she avoided doing anything directly. With the blindfold in place, my anticipation was heightened. Her mouth and hands and skin against me were enough to drive me wild. I gave up trying to remain silent, uncaring of what the passengers behind us could hear. My moans filled the space.

When I was teetering on the brink, Faith stopped.

"Wh-what?" I gasped, unable to manage anything more coherent.

"Patience." She stroked my arm, and I felt the first tingles of her *taaqat* enter me.

"Ohhh."

Faith's *taaqat* probed, then withdrew, pulling mine in its wake, the electric sparkles lighting my nerves.

Then she pushed it back into me, deeper, lingering, before drawing back again. I gasped as the wave flowed across my senses.

Again, diving deeper. Withdrawing again, my senses alight with pleasure. Again, again, again!

I was a wreck. I didn't know where she ended and I began, and I didn't care. With her final probe, she filled me, every inch of my being possessed by her, and I gave myself to her willingly, eagerly, knowing what approached.

Faith laid her lips on mine and pulled on both her *taaqat* and mine, emptying me, and I screamed. My orgasm rocked me, my muscles spasming, the fabric binding my wrists shredding. I was dimly aware of Faith's orgasm, an echo of mine, rippling through her, but only barely. When she collapsed onto me, I wrapped my newly freed arms around her and held her as we both panted.

"Good demon," she said when she'd recovered, sitting upright and straddling my middle. My recovery lagged, and I hoped she wouldn't demand too much of me.

"I try," I huffed.

She reached for my hands and placed them on her hips. "You broke your bonds, so you can do something useful with your freedom."

"Mistress." I stroked her sides, hearing her hiss in pleasure when I found a sensitive spot. I knew them all and spent blissful minutes building her anticipation. Faith moved around above me, presenting different angles to stroke, while adding her kisses in fresh places on my body.

"Now, my little demon, it's my turn."

I knew what she desired even before she brought her hips around to my mouth. In the years we had been together, we had tried everything Immortals could try. She'd even learned shapeshifting, and we'd played that way. But when Faith had to choose, she always went back to our first night together. Maybe it was sentimentality. Maybe it was a case of first learned, always preferred.

Whatever the reason, she wanted my mouth on her pussy.

"You changed your trim," I said, noting the petite heart made of her blonde curls, just above her folds, and the bare skin elsewhere. One benefit to shapeshifting was we never had to shave, simply willing the hair in or out of existence.

"I thought you might need some guidance." She snickered, voice muffled by my red curls.

"Guidance? As if." To prove it, I pressed my lips directly on her clit. She was so close to the edge that my one touch sent her over again.

Then I got serious.

I spent a blissful time caressing her with my mouth and my tongue, tasting her sweet, earthy ambrosia, a flavor I'd never known before her and found nowhere else. And one I never tired of.

I don't know how many times she came. Or how many times I did. Our bond amplified orgasms, a sort of erotic echo chamber, and when one of us climaxed, the other would almost invariably climax too.

Eventually, though, we were sated. It would be brief; it always was. But perhaps we could last the rest of the flight.

That's when I noticed a presence.

Faith.

She was resting, eyes closed, in the seat next to me, cuddled into my arm, the tail I occasionally manifested wrapped around her waist, her hand resting possessively over. *What?*

Someone's here.

A thrill of alarm flashed through her, then ebbed. *So? We'll handle it.*

I opened my eyes.

Crap.

"Melinda."

The stewardess had apparently missed the memo to give us privacy, and Faith hadn't pulled the curtain. She was staring at us, eyes wide with delighted fascination.

"I rather thought you might be sympathetic to my relationship with Gillian," she said. "I'm quite relieved to see I was correct. But a question, if I may?"

I didn't feel I was in a position to deny her request, but I couldn't think of any question which wasn't answered by the scene before her. "Yes?"

"Is that a tail?" Melinda pointed.

See? The answer was right in front of her. "Yes."

"Then you're not human." It wasn't a question, so I didn't need to answer. I did anyway.

"No."

"Is Faith?"

"No, I'm not." Faith had followed the conversation and jumped in.

"Ah." Melinda took a moment to process this. "Aliens? Like those terrible movies?"

"No, no aliens, and don't take us to your leader," I joked, and Faith buried her head in my shoulder, embarrassed. I loved the science fiction movies that were coming out. She hated them.

"Then what are you?"

"I'm a demon, and she's an angel." It might not have been entirely accurate, but it was easier than trying to explain the errors in nearly two thousand years of Western theology while my lover's juices were on my lips.

"Retired," Faith added.

"So you're not after my soul?"

I chuckled. "No."

"And you're not tempting me?"

"Not intentionally."

"Then why are you here?"

Turning on her most winning smile, Faith said, "Do you mind if we clean up and get dressed? Then we'll be happy to chat with you."

Melinda seemed to remember that we were naked and sexually sated. "Oh, yes, quite." She bustled off.

As we set about putting ourselves, and the cabin, to rights, I said, "Now what?"

"Now we get dressed."

"Faith...!"

"What? We talk to her. She's mortal, Kalili. What's more, she's been possessed by an archdemon. I think we can talk to her, and answer her questions if we can. It's better to tell the truth and recruit the mortals into keeping our secrets than to pretend it never happened. We've learned that lesson." She set the table back in place and willed the steel to reattach.

I winced. We had. The hard way. Humans would always fill in the unknown with speculation; the fewer facts they had, the wilder the stories got.

"Fine. You still owe me a new suit." I shapeshifted myself back into order, clothes and all.

"Yes, dear. I'll order one as soon as we get home." She dimpled, and I knew she was thinking something wicked.

"What?" I prompted, taking her into my arms.

"Well. I was thinking."

"That's what worries me."

"What are we going to do in Rome to top this?"

I laughed, then kissed her. "We'll think of something."

Afterward

So. That happened.

This little adventure ties up one of the many dangling threads from *Godsfall: The Book of One*—because even immortals deserve a vacation, and sometimes those vacations involve exorcisms, ruined suits, and unexpected stewardess-related drama.

It's also a reminder that Kalili and Faith aren't *always* trying to interfere in human affairs, reshape cosmic destiny, or save the damn world. Sometimes they're just trying to get from New York to Rome without attracting divine or demonic attention. (Spoiler: they usually fail. Spectacularly.)

At its core, *A Roman Holiday* is a love story. Not the kind that ends in marriage and a white picket fence—unless the fence is enchanted and the marriage involves blood oaths and celestial bureaucracy—but the kind where two very old beings still surprise each other, still love fiercely, and still have no idea how to cook pork chops.

Yes, this story fits neatly into the larger Cassidyverse—but it's a detour, not a roadmap. A side quest. A sexy, snarky, occasionally stabby layover in the middle of eternity.

Where should you go next?

If you're here for the sex, the sparks, the cosmic snark, and the origin of it all, *The Book of One* is your ticket. You'll find the first two chapters waiting for you right after this.

But if you're more curious about how Kalili and Faith navigate the human world with all its messy, mortal complications? *The Vault & The Vixen* is where they really start blending in (or trying to), while still occasionally smiting things.

However you found this little nugget of goodness, thank you for reading. Immortality's better with company—and we're glad you came along for the ride.

The best way to keep up with my work is at adamgaffenauthor.com[1] and through the biweekly newsletter Kendra insists on writing. I'm also around the Meta socials, Twitter/X, and at as many conventions as I can get to—if you see me, come say hi.

Until next time,

Adam Gaffen

Cassidyverse Air, Flight No. 13, now departing.

"Writing is antisocial. It's as solitary as masturbation. Disturb a writer when he is in the throes of creation and he is likely to turn and bite right to the bone... and not even know that he's doing it. As writers' wives and husbands often learn to their horror...There is no way that writers can be tamed and rendered civilized. Or even cured. In a household with more than one person, of which one is a writer, the only solution known to science is to provide the patient with an isolation room, where he can endure the acute stages in private, and where food can be poked in to him with a stick. Because, if you disturb the patient at such times, he may break into tears or become violent. Or he may not hear you at all... and, if you shake him at this stage, he bites..."

– Robert A. Heinlein

---

1. https://adamgaffenauthor.com

Preview of Godsfall: The Book of One

GODSFALL
THE BOOK OF ONE
ADAM GAFFEN

Warning

"Godsfall: The Book of One" contains violence, explicit sex, nudity, inappropriate use of church property, portrayals of beings divine and demonic bearing little or no resemblance to established religion or mythology, trespassing, bad language, sacrilege, blasphemy, attempted murder, arguable murder, divinely mandated attempted murder, justifiable murder, sexual promiscuity, kidnapping, attempted rape (which is never comedy), theft, assault and battery, panties, even more explicit sexuality, polyamory, abuse of authority, corruption of would-be popes, abuse of imps, uncomfortable discussions with exes, disturbances of the peace, disorderly conduct, mayhem, dismemberment, a completely different Trinity, more bad language, corruption of a minor, debauchery, gratuitous nudity, improper disposal of bodily fluids, blatant disregard for authority, and shagging. If any of this disturbs you, you should probably put the book down.

Now.

Prologue

New York City, today

"NO. DAMN IT, KALILI, we don't have to answer any of these stupid fucking requests!"

I tried not to sigh. When Faith was in one of her moods, there was no persuading her. Still, in over a millennium, I hadn't given up trying, and I wasn't going to stop now.

"Sweetheart," I started in my most dulcet tones.

"No, Kal. I know what you're trying to do, and why. And I'll even agree that maybe, just maybe, there's a point to Lilith's Chief of Staff asking for a formal record of our first weeks together." She waved a piece of parchment at me. Yes, honest-to-goodness parchment. Some things never changed.

"But now?" She crossed her arms over her chest. "Why now? Don't you find it a little suspicious?"

"No. Not really, not coming from her," I answered. "If it were Lucifer? Father of Lies, and he earned the title. But he didn't, she did. Besides, it's been over a thousand years. If not now, when? And I don't know about you, but I could use something new to do."

I swept my arm around the penthouse. Evidence of our recent occupations littered every surface. Being immortal, we'd had plenty enough time to find what we liked, practice it, master it, and get bored.

We were recycling hobbies now.

It was that or take an active role in the administration of the cosmos, and neither of us were overly interested. Don't get me started on the paperwork involved!

All of which meant we had plenty of time on our hands.

I extended my arm. "Give it to me." She handed it over without a protest.

I read it aloud. "Faith and Kalili." I stopped. "Why is your name first?"

The laugh I was gifted with was typical of Faith: light, airy, full of good humor, and one of my favorite things about her.

"No idea, love. Keep reading."

"Faith and Kalili. You are hereby requested to provide to this office a complete account of the events of, blah, blah, blah." I looked up. "Did you read the PS?"

"Of course I did."

I resumed reading. "*PS, You wouldn't believe the wild stories that go around about you two. I'd love to straighten them out with the facts. Can you clear it up for me? -A.*" Now I shrugged. "Seems like a pretty good reason to me. If we're going to be legends, we may as well be accurate legends."

Faith pursed her lips and exhaled.

"Fine. But you're doing it."

"Why me?" I protested.

Faith walked to me and put her arms over my shoulders. My arms went about her middle, almost of their own volition.

"First, because you're so much better at bureaucratic bullshit than I am."

She leaned in and kissed my neck, pulling ever so gently with her teeth.

"Second, because you remember it better than I do. I was pretty dazed for most of that first couple of weeks. You know, wide-eyed and petrified?"

Faith stretched so her lips brushed my earlobe, and I shivered.

"Third, you still owe me."

I pulled back a few inches. "For what?"

"You want a list, or do you trust me?"

Damn. She had me there.

"I trust you, my *arima bikia*." As always, when I used the celestial phrase for soulmate, our *taaqats* connected and we were One. It was a fraction of a second, but it was eternity.

"I know." Her voice was whisper soft.

"Okay, fine, I'll get started on it, but I'm writing it my way. All the things we took for granted, I'm going to explain. The shit we learned on the way? That too. Whatever I write, it's going to sound like I talk now, and it's gonna be in English, not Latin. I can't even remember all the flourishes and flowery shit I had to use when talking to nobles." I tried to pull away, but Faith's arms locked behind my neck.

"Not so fast, Kalili. I saw those wicked, wicked thoughts."

She grinned, and I grinned back.

"And?" I asked.

"And I have some improvements on them."

Fuck it. Paperwork could wait.

Faith came first.

Well, not always.

But that's another part of the story.

1 Kalili 1:1[1]

Rome, 952 AD

I was bored.

"Harder, Octavianus!" I said, and if my voice didn't carry the expected passion, well, my teenage lover didn't notice.

"That's right, oh, yes!"

I suppressed a yawn, then let it out anyway.

Not like he's going to see.

Octavianus was behind me, thrusting for all he was worth, my skirt tossed onto my back.

I hope he finishes soon.

My mind wandered. Demons weren't supposed to be bored. At least, Below would have me believe that. I wasn't entirely sure.

The problem? Immortality.

Demons are eternal unless someone kills us. Tough to do, yes, but possible. Too many people equate immortal with invulnerable, but that's not accurate.

The point is, unless something stops us, we keep going.

The same is true for angels, in case you were wondering.

It makes sense. We come from the same stock, created simultaneously, and set loose in the universe. Don't believe the bullshit about demons being angels that fell. The original Immortals, greater demons like me? Lucifer created us to oppose the Head Office.

All part of the fucked up ineffable plan.

It wasn't particularly relevant at that moment, except it made living through each day Earthside tedious in the extreme.

Having an unfamiliar task would have helped, but demons are notorious for having two kinds of luck: bad, and none.

I was still on the fence which type this assignment was. My mission was to seduce one of a half-dozen prospective Popes.

Been there, done that. This century, even.

"Sway him from his religious beliefs into a life of sin, then use your powers to shorten his life before he can resume a path which will lead him to chastity."

Blah, blah, blah.

What made this one worse was that Below hadn't done their research.

As usual.

Octavianus, son of Alberic II of Spoletto, was anything but chaste when I entered his life.

So much for swaying him, but I was stuck with the task.

Frankly, I didn't see the point. A corrupt pope or cardinal would be immeasurably more valuable to Below than one who failed to be selected and died.

Eh. What did I know?

He grunted at an especially hard thrust, and for a split second I hoped he was done. He resumed his pounding, dashing my hopes.

If I was human, I'd be sore in the morning.

I wriggled, hoping the additional stimulation would speed the process.

A minute later, he was still going strong. Time for me to play dirty.

"Don't stop, Van," I moaned. "Right there, don't stop, don't stop!"

Two thrusts later, Octavianus let out an impassioned groan and came.

Finally.

"Oh, lover, that was so good."

I didn't know if he heard me and didn't care. He pulled out of me and slapped my ass.

"You're a good fuck, Dora."

Right. My name for this assignment? I was Theodora, not Kalili, proving someone Below had a really crappy sense of humor. "Beloved of God" indeed! And what was wrong with Kalili? Perfectly neutral name, if unusual in Rome.

"You are a magnificent lover, Octavianus." I stood, allowing the fabric to fall over my legs. I'd clean up when I returned to my chambers.

At least you don't take much of my time.

He waved a hand in dismissal, and I fled.

First stop, bath. After that? I didn't have a clue. Which brought me full circle.

I was bored.

Don't get me wrong, boredom beat overwhelm all to hell, and I didn't lack for work. Rome was a cesspit of debauchery, and the closer you got to seats of power, the worse the stench.

Which was good for me and my companions. There were dozens of demons, Succubi, and incubi in Rome this spring. Agapetus II was ill again, and the jockeying for his successor had resumed. Which meant corruption season was in full swing.

But it was deathly dull, especially for a demon who had been around since the beginning of so-called civilization.

"Oh, bless it all!" I cursed.

"Problems, Kalili?" came a greasy voice behind me.

He thought he was oh-so-sneaky, but I had picked up on his aura and didn't show my surprise when he spoke.

"No, Coronatus."

Coronatus pouted.

He was an imp. Specifically, he was my imp. Think of him as a demonic secretary and you wouldn't be far off. As the senior demon on this assignment, he was tasked with keeping my appointments and handling schedules.

Did you know Hell invented paperwork?

Original in triplicate was one of their proudest moments.

And imps were masters of minutiae.

Short version? He was a pain in my ass.

Like other Immortals, Cor could make himself invisible. Unlike demons and angels, he couldn't make himself insubstantial, so while I could walk through walls if I wanted, he had to find doors.

I'm not saying I ever took advantage of this.

"Finished so soon? Did he commit to marrying you?"

That was my plan, such as it was. Get Van to marry me, since Below's scanty reports suggested he was most likely to be the successor. He was already corrupt, but a married cardinal would be challenged to become pope.

I'd only been working this angle for a few weeks, far too little time for any results, and Coronatus knew it. He was asking me just to be a prick.

Fine. I could be a prick, too, even without shapeshifting.

I passed through the door without him and smirked until he caught up.

"No, he fucked me and I left. He was already thinking about lunch and the serving boy. Not exactly the right time to ask. Besides, with him dripping down my leg, I didn't think it was romantic enough."

Demons and angels are touch-telepaths. When we're in contact with a human, or another immortal of equal or lower status, we can read their mind. It made my job easier, as it did for the Succubi. But eww. The things I saw in human minds could curdle the stomach of even the most experienced demon.

"Do you have an estimated date, Kalili?" I'll give him credit: he was persistent.

"No, I don't, and you can tell Below to stop asking me." I was feeling the pressure from Below. According to my orders? This was supposed to be a straightforward job. Again, they didn't do their research. If they had, they would have known that the potential of a papacy was enough of a lure to keep most mortals from taking a permanent entanglement, no matter how tempting. I had an outstanding track record, but wasn't infallible.

"I'll pass it along." Cor made a notation on the slate tablet. "Did you know there's a new angel in town?"

"I'd heard," I said. Angels came and went like cockroaches. I paid most of them as little attention.

"And she's assigned to watch you."

I yawned. Entirely staged. There was always an angel watching me.

No, it wasn't ego, or not entirely.

I was a very senior demon. Sure, there were older demons, and higher-ranking ones, but I'd been on Earth continuously for six millennia, and had been there and done that. It was a rare assignment that I didn't have one angel or another looking over my shoulder and trying to screw with me. I would be more surprised if I didn't have an angel I had to dodge.

So, new angel? So what? I smirked, seeing another wall ahead I could phase through to piss him off. Three more steps, two...

"And she's got permission to kill you."

My head snapped to the side and I walked into the wall.

"Fuck! Ow! What did you say?" I rubbed my injured shoulder.

"My source says she's ordered to kill you."

This was unusual.

Hugely so.

There was an unwritten détente between the two sides. Demons didn't kill angels, and angels didn't kill demons. Inconvenience? Absolutely. Interfere? Definitely. Injure? Sure, if we thought we could get away with it. But kill?

No!

We were immortal, but not invulnerable. A human could kill our bodies if they got lucky. Poison didn't work on us, neither did drowning nor smothering, or at least it never had before. Enough damage and we'd die, like a beheading, or multiple stab wounds. Shit like that. Unfortunately for them, that was little more than an irritating bunch of paperwork. We'd come back eventually and get our revenge.

Demons couldn't kill other demons. Not permanently.

I didn't know if angels could kill angels. I'd never cared enough to ask.

Only a demon could kill an angel forever, and vice versa.

The last demon killed by an angel was Gard, just over two centuries earlier. In fairness to the angel, it was totally justified. Gard went rogue, chopping wings off angels whenever he could. Wings, we didn't touch. Wings didn't grow back or heal, and while it would be a major inconvenience for any Immortal? It was awfully close to violating the détente.

The bosses Below worried that he'd escalate the Celestial War all on his own. His archdemon had tried to stop him, to no avail, and so Below quietly let it be known Gard was fair game, no longer protected.

He was the only one this millennium.

"Why? When?"

Cor shrugged. "Don't know. Do you want me to find out?"

I smacked his shoulder. "Yes!" What a stupid fucking question.

He smirked at me. "What's in it for me?"

I didn't have time for this. If an angel was searching for me, I needed information now, not later.

"Besides your continued existence?"

"You can't kill me." Which wasn't quite true. I could, but Below would issue him a new body and send him back to pester me. Then there was the paperwork, and probably a reprimand to go with it. To top it off, he'd be even more annoying when he returned.

This, I knew from hard-earned experience.

"A weekend off."

"A week."

"Three days."

"Four."

"Deal." I cursed myself inwardly. I shouldn't have negotiated downward, but it was a habit. A week free of him? Bliss! "After I get the information."

"Agreed." He stopped, forcing me to stop with him. "Sign."

"You don't trust me?" I was already reaching for the contract. An imp trusting a demon? Not likely. He snatched it back as soon as I'd made my mark and turned to walk away.

"Hey!"

"What?"

"Who is it? Do we know her?"

He shook his greasy black hair at me.

"No. At least I don't know her."

"Does she have a name?"

"Faith." Cor walked off. I wasn't getting any more from him today.

"Faith."

1 Kalili 1:2

I laid low for the rest of the day, ditching Octavianus and his return engagement. I was supposed to find him for an afternoon session, probably a suck-and-fuck, but staying alive seemed far more important. There might be repercussions for distancing myself from my target, but if I was dead?

I'd take the paperwork.

With Cor off on errands and investigating, I was cut off from my usual source of information. Anathia, a Succubus who was playing the role of my servant, didn't have the same connections as Cor.

I sent her off anyway.

What choice did I have?

I needed information. I needed it now, and she was better than nobody.

Specifically, I needed to know why I was on the Head Office's "Better Off Dead" list. What had I done, if anything? Or was this a larger offensive aimed at Below?

Who was Faith? Did anyone know her?

And how the fuck was I going to keep myself intact?

I paced my room while I tried to think, muttering as I did so.

"It's got to be attached to my assignment. That means Van is more important than I think, but why? He's a teenager! What else could it be? Is there anything? Think, Kal, think! What?" I snapped, hearing a sound and assuming it to be Anathia.

"Who is Kal?"

Shit. Octavianus.

I spun and pasted a smile on my face.

"Van!" I said in the brightest tone I could manage.

"Who is Kal?" he repeated with a hint of menace. Teenage humans were always prone to jealousy, whether male or female. I'd inspired enough to recognize the symptoms.

"Kal?" Maybe I could play dumb. He certainly was.

"Kal. Is this another lover?" His hand dropped to the knife he always wore.

"Oh, no, there's nobody else!" Much as it galled me, I told him the truth, and I hoped he could hear it. "I was just talking to myself. Bad habit." It certainly was, as I was being reminded now. "It's, ah, Arabic. Another way to say think."

Maybe it was lame, but it was the best I could come up with on short notice.

Fortunately, Octavianus's education was as spotty as his face.

"Kal. Hmm. 'Kal, you idiot!' I like it." He smiled, but then it faded. "Where were you earlier?"

Maybe I was worried about the angel, but I'd prepared for this question.

"I'm sorry. I had a headache and sent Coronatus to tell you. Did he not? I'll have him beaten."

"No, he didn't. And I will have him killed for failing to pass along your message!" Typically dramatic teenage shit, all bluster and no substance. He was no more likely to set anyone to kill Cor than he was to stop seeing me.

I knew what he wanted to hear, so I said it.

"As you wish."

He seemed mollified, and I started thinking again. The only reason an angel would be assigned to kill me was if Van was important. If he was important, she'd be keeping track of him and his movements. If she were tracking him, she'd follow him...

Here!

Fuck.

I had to get him out of here, and fast. She could appear any moment!

An angel wouldn't hesitate to attack a demon, even in front of a human, no matter the harm it might do to their fragile brain. They had rules against it, of course. They had rules against everything, or so I'd heard. Slaying a demon, though, trumped the rule book.

I didn't care about the potential damage to Octavianus's worldview, but I didn't need him getting in my way if I had to fight for my life. He had to go, and the best way to do that was to give him what he wanted. At the very least, I had to get him to stop thinking.

The surest way to shut off his brain?

Send the blood to his other head.

I closed the gap between us and ran my hands along his legs. He was properly dressed, a tunic that ran down to mid-thigh and hose, but he never fastened the hose correctly. It was a simple matter for my hands to creep over the top and find him half-erect in anticipation.

Or perhaps just the normal teenage hormones.

Either way, I could work with it.

"Oh, Van," I purred. "You brought me a gift. How thoughtful!"

In the weeks I had been his lover, he had never once refused my mouth, and he didn't now. When he'd finished, as I wiped my lips with the back of my hand, he cuffed my shoulder.

"That's for missing this afternoon," he said, trying for gruff and missing by a lifetime.

"It was?" I simpered. "My apologies. Though we could do this more often." I added a purr to my voice. *It's a damn sight easier and faster than taking you to bed!*

"Perhaps." He lifted me to my feet. If he'd had a chance, he might have been a decent person. Flashes of the man he could have become showed occasionally.

It was almost a pity.

"Tonight. Here. Don't be late." He stared into my eyes.

I dropped my gaze to the floor. "I won't."

He left, almost slamming the door after him. I found a bottle and drank from the neck. Yuck. He needed more fruit in his diet and less garlic.

With Van handled for now, I could return to the more pressing issue of a murderous angel.

If this Faith was hunting me, then it was at the explicit direction of the Head Office. Angels simply didn't take the initiative, always reacting to what we did. They could act to thwart a demon when we were sloppy enough to be noticed. But escalating to violence?

Only on orders.

And I was back to the beginning.

I was a pain in the ass, yes, but I knew my place. Despite my experience, I wasn't high enough in the Lowerarchy to make a difference if they took me off the board.

It was infuriating!

I didn't even have a description of this angel, so I couldn't watch out for her.

Anathia, where the fuck are you?

Right. Rational. Logic. Figure this shit out.

Angels couldn't change their forms, so if she was female, she'd appear female. Or rather, they could, since they were the same stock as demons, and we could. But the Head Office had rules against it, and those pricky-shit, goody-two-shoes, do-gooders wouldn't dare break a rule.

Pussies.

Problem. There were dozens of women who worked at the palace on the Via Lata, and I only knew a few of them by sight.

If she were smart—and having an Earthside assignment suggested she was—she'd be hiding her aura, so I couldn't reliably spot her that way.

Damn and blast.

I dropped onto a couch with a thump.

This sucked.

I continued this unprofitable line of thought for some time until I realized the afternoon had slipped away. I barely had enough time to change for the evening meal. It wouldn't do to be late, but I couldn't arrive in my comfortable clothes. In the end, I shapeshifted a new outfit into existence, along with makeup and hairdo. It cost me *taaqat*, celestial energy, but it was my own damn fault.

I zombied my way through dinner, putting my body on automatic and going through the motions of polite conversation. Every sense was on alert, seeking the slightest trace of her aura, the holier-than-thou stench that the angels couldn't help but generate.

Nothing.

I realized I might have been a bit too distracted when one of Octavianus's cronies took my hand and tried to lead me from the room.

"Get off me!"

I might have screamed it. Maybe. That would explain why everyone went silent.

"Theodora." He used *that* tone. You know the one.

The let's not make a fuss tone always set my teeth on edge. Still does, which shows how little things change.

He tugged on my hand, expecting me to follow.

I slapped him.

"You said you would!" he said, rubbing his cheek. I didn't have to be psychic to know what he meant. While normally I wouldn't mind draining a few months from his life, I really didn't have time today, and zero interest.

Still, every eye in the hall was on us now, and I did *not* need to be the center of attention.

I needed time to regroup, so I temporized. "I didn't mean tonight."

"That's not what you said a moment ago."

"Dionisio." Was that his name? Probably. He reacted like it was. "I misunderstood. I'm sorry."

He didn't react badly, so I took the chance to sidle close to him, taking his hands in mine. "But I'll make it up to you tomorrow. I promise."

The promise of a demon is worth the parchment it's written on, but he believed me. I felt it and had a flashing image of what he intended to do with me. It was definitely sinful and would subtract at least two months from his life.

"I will come for you at dinner." He bowed over my hand before I released him.

"Until tomorrow." I put as much desire into my voice as I could, enhanced by my reputation as Octavianus's favorite, and he finally left.

I'd had enough as well and retreated to my rooms. Maybe Anathia had returned with information.

When I arrived, Anathia was still missing, and I snarled curses. Of course, I'd forgotten to give her a deadline. While she wouldn't *not* bring me the information, eventually, she probably wouldn't put any urgency on it. If she could drain some life from her sources? She'd probably see it as a win-win.

I was so busy considering my next moves I failed to notice the figure emerge from my bedchamber until she cleared her throat.

Fuck me.

It was the angel.

"Demon."

She was glowing. I saw right through it, since it was one of the stupid parlor tricks the Head Office bestowed upon their feckless minions to create a sense of awe in the unaware. I could see it for what it was, and see through it.

Faith was in full regalia, as defined by the popular human perception of angels. Unimaginative lot. She could have appeared in anything, but no. Short white tunic, loosely belted with a golden rope, sandals, a gladius to do the deed, and wings.

Yeah, wings. Which meant her tunic had some major alterations. I wasn't sure why she bothered. If she was trying to impress me, there were other ways to do it. Intimidate me? Unlikely, since I had a pair just as wide.

I shooed away the idle thought. This was an angel sent to kill me.

Then I saw *her*, under the glitz and glamour.

She was tall, nearly as tall as me, maybe an inch less than my five feet six inches, blonde where I was red, lithe and lean, with skin the color of honeyed oak. Her eyes were copper-colored, instead of my green, and were blazing with righteous fury. It was her lips that caught me, lips pressed together in anger and determination, lips I wanted nothing more than to kiss.

Wait.

Kiss?

What the Hell was wrong with me?

"Kalili, Demon of the Pit."

Her harsh tone jerked me out of the hormone-induced haze and I started thinking above the waist.

I knew what she was doing. It was their idiotic rules again. She couldn't strike me down immediately. She had to pronounce the sentence against me and give me an opportunity to depart. Something was off, and when I thought about it, I realized what it was.

Her voice was hard, but it was brittle, unsure.

This angel wasn't familiar with Earth, or demons, and only had her training and instructions to go on. She might be smart enough to win an Earthside assignment, but she was inexperienced. I was in with a chance.

"You have sinned against the Way. Your existence is forfeited. But We are merciful, and if you flee this world, never to return, We will postpone your judgment until the End Times."

I knew what she was saying, and I should have been running while she nattered.

I couldn't. Her voice was captivating, melodious despite the dire threats it carried.

What was I thinking?

I didn't know. But I wasn't moving, not as long as she was speaking, even though she was talking about my death.

She stopped, reaching the end of her memorized speech, and I realized she was *terrified!* My brain snapped back on, and I shook off the lethargy of the past minute.

"Hey, hold on." I smiled as winningly as I knew how. "Can we talk about this? Isn't there supposed to be a trial?"

"We have judged you." She took a step toward me, sword at the ready, the tip quivering. Anticipation or nerves? I was betting on nerves.

I thought about her words. They didn't sound right. Yes, demons were guilty, simply by serving Below. A judgement, though, implied a trial, and a trial required specific crimes. Otherwise, the game would be entirely different.

"By whom?" I demanded, and she stopped.

"What?" She sounded puzzled.

"Who judged me?"

She responded with a question. "Demon, who are you to doubt me?"

"We doubt everything." Stall, stall! I shuffled away from her, thinking furiously. "Who are you to be executing a sentence?"

"I am Faith, of—"

I cut her off, putting as much scorn into my voice as I could.

"Hold on. I don't care what angelic choir group you belong to, Faith. Who told you to kill me?"

"I, what?" She shook her head to clear it of the confusion I had planted. "We have judged you."

"You said that. Who? Where's my notice? You can't try me without telling me I'm on trial. It's part of your rules."

It was. Hell may have invented bureaucracy and paperwork, but the Head Office adopted it pretty damn fast, and they were even more rule-bound than we were. At least demons always knew to look for loopholes, and negotiate, and try any of a thousand tricks.

Angels followed the letter of the command.

Maybe I could use that against her. It seemed to work so far.

"Listen, Faith." I kept edging toward my desk. I kept a dagger hidden under the parchments, and if I couldn't talk her out of this fool's errand, well... Going down fighting was a better option.

"I'm not going to argue the case, because *I don't know anything about it!* I'm supposed to, right? It's in your rules, isn't it? I have to have my day in court, my chance to answer? Why don't you go find out what happened, and maybe we can get this all cleared up?"

I saw the doubt and knew I'd won a reprieve, even if she didn't know it yet.

"Seriously, Faith. I know we're not friends. We just met, but I know your side follows the rules."

"Because you don't!" she bellowed.

"We get creative," I admitted. "Killing me is a pretty drastic step, don't you think?"

"I—yes, it is." The tip of the gladius, still quivering, drooped.

"Good. Then go get your little piece of parchment, or your Archangel, or someone who can clear all this up. Eh?"

"Oh, bless it all!" She threw the gladius to the ground and dropped to the floor.

I can't explain what happened next, certainly not using the understood roles of angels and demons. If I were truly the wretched and evil creature she claimed I was, I would have pounced on the sword. I might have even lopped off her head.

Instead, to both our surprises, I kicked it away from us and caught her almost before she hit.

I found my arms full of weeping angel.

What the fuck?

My rational brain was telling me to pull away, let her stay on the floor, and run.

A tiny part of me took over and made me stay.

She needs you, it whispered. *You belong here, her body warm against you.*

What the hell.

At least I didn't burst into flame. I didn't think I would, but then again, I'd never held an angel.

I don't know how long it was before she spoke.

"M-M-Michael will be so angry with me!" She was sobbing into my tunic, and I really hoped Octavianus would be delayed. A glowing woman with wings in the arms of his lover? That might be a little too challenging to explain.

Then I recognized whose name she'd said. An Archangel ordered my death? Oh, Kalili, you really pissed in someone's punch this time.

"Did Michael give the order?" I didn't know too much about how their hierarchy worked, but everyone knew Michael was in charge of what they laughably called justice.

Maybe it was sneaky, taking advantage of her when she was vulnerable.

Sue me.

I'm a demon.

"It came from his office, his seal," she said with a nod. "I have to report back to him when—when—"

She realized where she was then and leaped to her feet.

"What are you doing?!"

"Keeping your ass from hitting the floor," I snapped, the spell broken again. I rose, quickly but not hurriedly, and pointed at the door. "Get out."

"I will! And when I return, Kalili the Demon, I will strike you down!"

She pivoted and stomped away, vanishing as she passed through the wall.

Dramatic exit. I'd give her that.

I shook my head in disbelief. Had I just talked my way out of a death sentence? At least for now?

Without warning, she reappeared, cheeks aflame.

"My sword," she said in explanation, finding it and scooping it from under my chair. Then she did her trick and vanished again.

I couldn't help it. I laughed.

When Octavianus returned a half-hour later, I didn't even mind.

---

[1] A note on chapters in this book. They are meant to be read as you would a biblical chapter. So this would be First Kalili One One. You'll see why.

Don't miss out!

Visit the website below and you can sign up to receive emails whenever Adam Gaffen publishes a new book. There's no charge and no obligation.

https://books2read.com/r/B-A-PBTN-CCVBD

Connecting independent readers to independent writers.

Did you love *A Roman Holiday*? Then you should read *The Vault & The Vixen*[1] by Adam Gaffen!

[2]

Is the heist of a lifetime worth her heart?

Dive into the heart-pounding world of The Vault & the Vixen, where heist thriller meets romantic suspense in a gripping tale of crime, love, and redemption. Set against the gritty, neon-lit backdrop of Brooklyn, this novel weaves a complex web of high-stakes heists, intricate plots, and unyielding loyalty.

Meet Dakota Chase, a master planner and the fearless leader of a crew that specializes in pulling off the impossible. With her long dark hair and iconic leather coat, Dakota is the epitome

---

1. https://books2read.com/u/4Ed92Y

2. https://books2read.com/u/4Ed92Y

of cool, collected, and cunning. She's spent years navigating the treacherous waters of organized crime, always staying one step ahead of both the law and her rivals. But as she gears up for the heist of a lifetime, the stakes have never been higher.

Dakota's meticulous plans are put to the test as unforeseen complications arise, and betrayal lurks around every corner. Her crew, a tight-knit group of skilled misfits, stands by her side, each member bringing their unique talents to the table. New to the crew is McKenna, a tough-as-nails tech expert with short blonde hair and a penchant for plaid shirts. Their relationship is fraught with tension and unspoken feelings, and could throw a monkey wrench into Dakota's plan.

As Dakota and her team delve deeper into the underbelly of urban crime, they must confront powerful enemies, navigate dangerous alliances, and uncover secrets that threaten to tear them apart. The city of Brooklyn itself becomes a character in the story, its streets and shadows providing the perfect setting for the unfolding drama.

Will Dakota succeed in pulling off the ultimate heist, or will she find herself ensnared in a deadly game of cat and mouse? Can she trust her crew—and her heart—as she navigates the perilous world of organized crime? The Vault & the Vixen is a thrilling ride, packed with twists and turns, that will keep you on the edge of your seat until the very last page.

Tropes: Heist Thriller, Romantic Suspense, Crime Fiction, Urban Fiction, LGBTQ+ Fiction, Mastermind, Loyal Crew, Heist Gone Wrong, Enemies to Lovers, Forbidden Love, Gritty Urban Setting, Complex Characters, Plot Twists, High Stakes, Emotional Depth, Tension and Betrayal.

Join Dakota Chase on her electrifying journey through danger, deceit, and desire in The Vault & the Vixen. If you're a fan of edge-of-your-seat action, intricate plots, and deeply human stories, this is the book you've been waiting for!

Read more at www.adamgaffenauthor.com.

Also by Adam Gaffen

Godsfall
The Book of One
The Book of Two
The Book of Three
A Roman Holiday
Godsfall: Books 1-3
Sherlock Holmes and the Case of the Lazarus Conspiracy

Tales from the Cassidyverse
Into the Black
The Heart of Space
The Shape of the Fire
Midnight Relics

The Artemis War
The Road to the Stars
The Measure of Humanity
A Quiet Revolution

Triumph's Ashes

The Cassidy Chronicles
Run Like Hell
The Cassidy Chronicles - The Spark Before the Fire
Terran Federation Technical Manual
The Eternity Protocol: Complete Duology
Shades of Rose: Becoming
Shades of Rose: Breaking
The Girl in the Scope
Quantum Quirks: A Science Fiction Childhood
Embers of Eternity
Shades of Rose: Complete Duology

The Covenant
Shadow Bound

The Missions of the TFS Pike
The Ghosts of Tantor
Tracking Tantor

Standalone
The Kildaran
Roots of Love

Refuge
The Artemis Wars Omnibus
The Vault & The Vixen
Death Gets an Upgrade
Whispers in the Fog: Two Unpublished Holmes Mysteries
Dating to Die For

Watch for more at www.adamgaffenauthor.com.

About the Author

If you want strong FMCs who don't wait to be rescued, wit, and stories that will keep you up until 2am, then you're in the right place!

What *doesn't* Adam Gaffen write?

Well, hold on. He might be on it now.

So far his Cassidyverse contains Science Fiction, Fantasy, Thriller, and Rom-Com, with Dark Romance on the horizon.

He's a member of the Science Fiction Writers of America, and the Heinlein Society. He and his wife are owned by a pack of dogs and cats.

Read more at www.adamgaffenauthor.com.

www.ingramcontent.com/pod-product-compliance
Lightning Source LLC
Chambersburg PA
CBHW020629160726
47991CB00002B/957